Mystery Man

Bert moved to the side of Mr. Newman's house. Behind a curtain he saw a large shadow. "That can't be Mr. Newman," he whispered to himself. "Too short."

Next Bert heard three loud crashes that sounded as if furniture was being knocked over.

Now the curtains were moving wildly. Someone was behind them, desperately trying to yank them open!

A second shadow appeared. It was much taller than the first. The shadows looked as though they were fighting with each other.

All of a sudden, the figures fell to the ground with a tremendous crash!

Then there was complete silence.

Books in The New Bobbsey Twins series

Available from MINSTREL Books

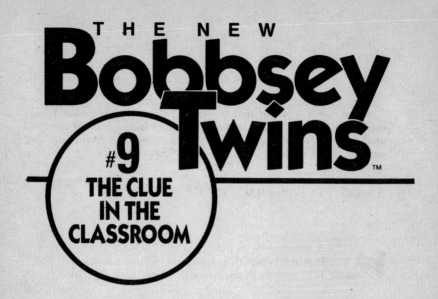

THE NEW
Bobbsey Twins
#9
THE CLUE IN THE CLASSROOM

LAURA LEE HOPE

ILLUSTRATED BY PAUL JENNIS

A MINSTREL® BOOK

PUBLISHED BY POCKET BOOKS

New York   London   Toronto   Sydney   Tokyo

A MINSTREL PAPERBACK *ORIGINAL*

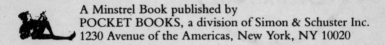

A Minstrel Book published by
POCKET BOOKS, a division of Simon & Schuster Inc.
1230 Avenue of the Americas, New York, NY 10020

Copyright © 1988 by Simon & Schuster Inc.
Cover artwork copyright © 1988 by Linda Thomas

Produced by Mega-Books of New York, Inc.

ISBN: 0-671-63072-5

First Minstrel Books printing December 1988

10 9 8 7 6 5 4 3 2 1

THE NEW BOBBSEY TWINS is a trademark
of Simon & Schuster Inc.

THE BOBBSEY TWINS, A MINSTREL BOOK and colophon
are registered trademarks of Simon & Schuster Inc.

Printed in the U.S.A.

Contents

THE CLUE
IN THE
CLASSROOM

1

Nan's New Teacher

"Bert, you're driving me crazy," said Nan Bobbsey. "Why don't you just walk down the sidewalk like a normal person? Why are you running from behind one tree to the next? Are you in training to be a squirrel or something?"

"No," her twelve-year-old twin brother replied. "I'm practicing to be a great detective." Bert pulled a comic book out of his pocket. "See how Rex Sleuther is following this guy in these pictures? He's staying a few feet behind him and hiding when he has to."

Nan rolled her eyes and ran her fingers through her brown hair. "You're going to make us late for school."

"We've got at least fifteen minutes. You go on ahead and let me practice following you. I'm getting real good at it. Even you won't see me."

"Okay, but this is the last time I'll do this with you on the way to school." Nan turned and headed down the street.

Bert followed at a distance, keeping a careful eye on his sister.

Suddenly Nan spun around.

Bert ducked into a doorway. He counted to ten. Then he peered out.

"Hey!" he shouted, when Nan jumped right in front of him. "No fair!"

"Shhh!" said Nan. "Something strange is going on across the street."

"What?"

"See that guy over there?" Nan pointed to a tall, thin man in a business suit. He was carrying a brown briefcase.

"What's so weird about him?"

"Just watch," she said as she joined Bert in the dark shadows of a storefront.

The tall man was standing across the street, about halfway down the block. He glanced nervously over his shoulder for a moment. Then he walked away quickly.

Ten seconds later he stopped in his tracks and quickly turned around.

2

"What's he doing?" asked Bert.

"I don't know, but he's been doing it all the way down the block. He walks a few feet, then stops and glances over his shoulder. See? There he goes again."

"He seems nervous," said Bert. "I wonder if he's a spy?"

The twins crept out of their hiding place. They continued down the block, then stopped behind a large mailbox.

The tall man suddenly ducked into a doorway and flattened himself against the glass door.

"He acts as if he's being followed," Bert said.

"You should know," said Nan, teasing her brother.

The man leapt out of the doorway, ran twenty yards, and ducked into another doorway.

"Weird," said Nan. "There's something going on here."

"Well, there's no evidence of a crime," Bert pointed out. "But we'll be in trouble ourselves if we're late for school."

Bert tucked his Rex Sleuther comic book inside his loose-leaf notebook.

"Hey!" exclaimed Nan. "Now look at that."

"Where?" asked Bert, looking over the mailbox. "I don't see anything."

Nan pointed. "A short guy in a tan trench coat is following the man with the briefcase."

"But he's just walking along the sidewalk."

"No," Nan replied. "Every time the tall man makes a move, the man in the trench coat stops to tie his shoe or look in a store window."

"You're right, Nan. This looks suspicious."

All of a sudden the tall man raced down the street. The short man in the trench coat quickly followed. Then the two men disappeared around the corner.

Nan and Bert left their hiding place and raced after the two men. But when the twins rounded the corner, they almost bumped into the man in the trench coat!

The short man wore very thick glasses and had stiff black hair that stood straight up. He frowned angrily as he scratched his head and looked up and down the street.

He turned toward the twins and stared at them with a strange expression. His thick glasses made his eyes seem very large. For a second it appeared as if he was going to come after them. But then he turned away and continued looking around.

Nan and Bert didn't say a word as they carefully walked past him. When they were out of earshot, Bert said, "Whew, I thought he was

going to grab us or something. That guy gives me the creeps."

"Me, too." Nan shivered. "There was something about his eyes, the way they were staring at us from behind those thick glasses."

"I sure won't forget that weird hair of his," Bert added. "It looked like a wire brush."

"But where did the tall man with the briefcase disappear to?" asked Nan.

Bert shrugged his shoulders. "How should I know?"

Suddenly they heard a horn honking. "Hey, Bert! Nan!" shouted their younger brother, Freddie, out the window of the family station wagon.

Mrs. Bobbsey pulled the wagon over to the curb. "Do you kids want a ride?" she asked.

"Sure," Nan answered. "If Freddie promises not to spill any ink on me like he did on himself and Flossie this morning."

"It was an accident," said Freddie. "I thought it was disappearing ink for writing secret messages. I must have grabbed the bottle of ink for my art project instead."

Freddie's twin sister, Flossie, groaned out loud. "You almost made us late because we had to change our clothes. My dress was ruined!"

Bert climbed into the car after Nan. He

ruffled Flossie's blond curls. "Come on, Floss. Freddie didn't do it on purpose."

Flossie ducked away from Bert's hand. "You boys always stick together," said Flossie, making a face.

A few minutes later, Mrs. Bobbsey drove up in front of the Lakeport Elementary School. That was Flossie and Freddie's school. The older twins went to the Lakeport Middle School, next door.

"Hurry up, kids. You've only got a minute before the bell rings," Mrs. Bobbsey said.

The two sets of twins piled out of the car and ran toward the redbrick buildings.

Nan's first class was science, and she didn't want to be late. Mrs. Kane, the old science teacher, had moved away the week before. Nan wanted to check out the new science teacher before class started.

When Nan entered the room there was a man standing behind the teacher's desk. The movie screen was pulled down on the wall behind him.

Nan looked at the man. Suddenly she had a strange feeling. She'd seen him before. But where?

Then she remembered! Sure enough, the

brown briefcase was next to his desk. He was the same tall, nervous man she and Bert had seen on the way to school that morning.

"Uh, are you the new teacher?" Nan asked.

"Yes," he said. "My name is Mr. Newman. Which student are you?"

"Nan Bobbsey," she replied.

Mr. Newman gave her a pleasant smile. "It's nice to meet you, Nan," he said.

Other students come into the classroom, and Nan took her seat. Nellie Parks, her best friend, sat down beside her and whispered, "Did you meet the new teacher?"

Nan nodded, but her mind was racing. Why would anyone follow a teacher to school? And why had Mr. Newman acted so nervous before? He didn't seem nervous now.

"Good morning, everyone," said the teacher. "I'm Mr. Newman, your new science teacher. Now, to introduce you to your first assignment I'll need to use the blackboard. Does anyone know how to roll up this movie screen? It was pulled down when I came in, and I can't seem to find the switch to raise it."

"I'll do it," yelled a boy in the back of the room. He went over to the light switch and pushed a small black button.

"Oh, that's where it is," said Mr. Newman. "Thank you." Then he sat down at his desk.

With a loud hum the large movie screen behind the teacher began rolling up into the ceiling. As the screen rose, the students could see the blackboard behind it. There were some words written there in bright yellow chalk.

"What's that on the blackboard?" Nellie whispered to Nan.

Mr. Newman was looking at his notes and didn't notice the strange message.

But as Nan began copying the message into her notebook, Danny Rugg, the meanest kid in school, called out, "Hey, Teacher. Give up your plans!"

Mr. Newman looked up from his desk. "What are you talking about?"

"How would I know?" Danny said. "Look behind you on the blackboard."

The teacher spun around and saw the message: "Newman, give up your plans. We're watching you."

"Oh no!" he cried. "They've found out! They know!"

2

Behind the Curtain

Everyone in the class stared as Mr. Newman jumped out of his chair and erased the message.

"What did he mean by 'they know'?" whispered Nellie. "Who is he talking about?"

"I have no idea," Nan whispered back.

Mr. Newman took a deep breath. Then he turned around and faced the class. He looked a little calmer. "Your first assignment will be an individual science project," he said. "Each student must choose a subject that has to do with living things."

"Can I study cars?" asked Charlie Mason.

"I said living things. Not mechanical things."

"What about live rock and roll?" Danny Rugg shouted. The class laughed.

Mr. Newman sighed. "That's *not* what I had in mind."

"Can I do something about plants?" asked Nan.

Mr. Newman nodded. "You can do projects about anything to do with plants or animals. Just have a three-D model or poster-size presentation finished in two weeks."

"Two weeks!" muttered Nellie Parks. "This guy is really tough."

"I've prepared a list of possible subjects," explained Mr. Newman. "But please feel free to come up with your own."

As the teacher handed out the papers, Nan thought about the message on the board. Why had Mr. Newman been so upset about it? she wondered. Did it have anything to do with the man in the trench coat?

After school, Nan walked home with Bert and the younger twins. Nan told Freddie and Flossie about the man she and Bert had seen that morning before school.

"And guess what?" she added. "He's my new science teacher, Mr. Newman!"

After she finished telling them about the message on the blackboard, Bert said, "I've got a hunch there's something suspicious about Mr. Newman. I think I'd better check him out."

"You always have a hunch," said Nan with a laugh.

"I like Mr. Newman," Freddie said.

"How do you know him?" Flossie asked.

"He came to my class this afternoon," Freddie answered. "He's going to teach the after-school science club, the one I signed up for. Tomorrow's the first meeting."

"That might be useful," said Nan. "Maybe you could help us learn more about this mysterious Mr. Newman."

"What's he like in class?" asked Bert. "Is he tough?"

"He gave us an assignment the first day, but it won't be too hard. We have to do a science project in two weeks. We can do it on plants or animals. I chose plants."

"Why don't you study dogs?" Flossie said. "You could use Chief for your project." Chief was the Bobbseys' sheepdog puppy.

"I don't think Mr. Newman would like it if I brought Chief to class," Nan said, smiling.

"I don't think Chief would like it, either," Freddie pointed out.

"That reminds me," Nan said. "Flossie, this is your day to feed Chief, right?"

"Wrong!" said Flossie. "It's *your* day."

Flossie and Nan began to argue over whose turn it was to feed Chief. Freddie and Bert moved away. "Let's get out of here," Freddie urged, looking at his two sisters.

"Good idea," said Bert. "Tell me, what are you going to be doing in this new science club?"

"We're going to learn all about science, especially robots," explained Freddie. "I can hardly wait until tomorrow. We're meeting at Mr. Newman's house to see some of his inventions."

"Where does Mr. Newman live?" asked Bert.

"He lives a few blocks away from our house," Freddie said. "Fifteen-oh-two Clearview Drive."

"Well, I'm going to take a look at Mr. Newman's house this afternoon," said Bert. "Maybe I'll find out something."

"That sounds like a good idea," said Freddie. "Can I help?"

"Sure," said Bert. He handed Freddie his books. "But not today. Tomorrow you can be the inside man. That means you'll be able to get information because you'll be inside Mr. Newman's house. After your science club meeting, you can tell us everything you've seen in there. We want to figure out why he's acting so weird."

"Okay," Freddie agreed. "But why do you want to look at Mr. Newman's house right now?"

"I have a hunch," said Bert. "And a good detective always follows his hunches."

"That's better than having your hunches follow you!" Freddie said jokingly. He ran off down the street toward the Bobbseys' house.

Bert walked to Mr. Newman's house, on Clearview Drive. The yellow house was surrounded by a white picket fence and four tall fir trees.

Bert saw a newspaper on the porch and a pile of mail stuffed in the mailbox. It looked as though Mr. Newman wasn't home from school yet.

Bert looked around the tree-lined street. There was nobody in sight. He vaulted over the picket fence and crept up to the side of the house.

All the curtains and shades on Mr. Newman's windows were pulled shut. Bert opened a small notebook. Writing in Rex Sleuther's secret code, he scribbled the time, address, and a note: XYP5EER, which meant no one was home.

Suddenly he saw a large shadow behind a curtain. "That can't be Mr. Newman," he whispered to himself. "Too short."

Bert quickly made a few more notes. Then, as he looked up, the person behind the curtain fell over backward!

"That's not Mr. Newman," said Bert. "So who is it?"

The person got up, but a second later, he or she fell over sideways.

Suddenly Bert heard footsteps coming from the front of the house. Then he heard a key turning in a lock. He peered around the side of the house. Mr. Newman was home from school.

Next Bert heard three loud crashes that sounded as if furniture was being knocked over. He looked back at the window.

The curtains were moving wildly. Someone was behind them, desperately trying to yank them open!

A second shadow appeared. It was much taller than the first. The shadows looked as thought they were fighting with each other.

All of a sudden, the two figures fell to the floor with a tremendous crash!

Then there was complete silence.

3

Uninvited Visitors

Bert raced around to the front of Mr. Newman's house.

"Is everything all right in there?" he shouted, knocking hard on the oak-paneled door.

There was no answer.

"Is anyone home?" yelled Bert, knocking again.

Footsteps came toward the door.

"Who is it?" asked a man's voice.

"Uh, Bert Bobbsey," he replied. "Is everything all right?"

The door opened a crack. Mr. Newman peered out. "Of course it is," he answered. Bert glanced past Mr. Newman. He couldn't see much because the inside of the house was dark.

"Is anyone else here?" Bert asked. "I heard some funny noises."

Mr. Newman smiled. "No, there's nobody else here. I live alone. Are you one of the students at Lakeport Middle School? Bobbsey . . . hmmm, I seem to remember meeting someone with that name today."

"That must have been my sister Nan," said Bert. "She's in your science class."

Mr. Newman opened the door a little wider. "Yes, you look like her."

"We're twins." Again Bert tried to peek inside the house. "Are you sure everything is all right?"

"Of course I'm sure," the teacher replied. There was a touch of irritation in his voice. "I'm sorry, but I'm very busy right now. Goodbye."

Mr. Newman closed the door, but Bert didn't leave. He was *sure* he'd seen a fight through the curtains.

Listening carefully, he couldn't hear any more sounds coming from inside Mr. Newman's house.

"Bert! Bert, where are you?"

He turned around and saw his younger sister, Flossie, racing down the street. Bert left Mr.

Newman's porch and headed out to the sidewalk.

"Freddie told me I could find you here," said Flossie, nearly out of breath.

"Is something wrong?"

"No, but there will be if you don't get home soon. Mom says you're supposed to be cleaning your room."

Bert snapped his fingers. "I'd forgotten that. Rats!"

"Good thing I found you, then," Flossie said. She looked at Mr. Newman's house. "Did you find out anything about Mr. Newman?" she asked in a low voice.

"Kind of," Bert said thoughtfully. "There's something—"

Before Bert could finish, a short woman with dark wavy hair came rushing up to the two Bobbseys. "Excuse me," she said. "May I speak with you for a moment?"

"Yes, ma'am," Bert said politely.

"Are you lost?" asked Flossie. "My brother knows every street in Lakeport."

The woman smiled. "No," she said. "I'm not lost. I live in Lakeport, too."

"What can we do for you?" asked Bert.

"I noticed you were talking to Mr. Newman a moment ago."

"Are you a friend of Mr. Newman's?" asked Bert.

"I'm Mrs. Julie Burns," she explained. "Mr. Newman used to work for me at DataComp Industries."

"That's a nice suit you're wearing," interrupted Flossie. "Pink is my favorite color, too."

"I'm glad you like it," Mrs. Burns replied, smiling. "But I'd like your brother to tell me more about Mr. Newman. Did you go into his house?"

"No," answered Bert. "He was too busy for visitors."

"That's too bad," Mrs. Burns said. She seemed disappointed. "I was hoping you might have seen something."

"Like what?" Bert asked.

"I can't say," said Mrs. Burns. She leaned in close to Bert and Flossie. "It's a matter of security. Very hush-hush."

"You mean like spies?" said Flossie, her blue eyes getting bigger by the second.

Julie Burns smiled at her. "I'm sorry, that's all I can say." With that she spun around and walked to a long black limousine that was pulling up to the curb. The limo stopped, and a heavyset bald man got out. He held the door open for Mrs. Burns.

"Let's go, Mr. Carroll," ordered Julie Burns.

21

"Another dead end." She got into the back of the limo.

Mr. Carroll slid in next to the driver. "Don't worry. Wait until—" The limousine door slammed shut, and the chauffeur sped away.

Bert shook his head. "A security matter," he said. "That sounds like spy talk to me."

"I don't like that Mr. Carroll," Flossie said with a shiver. "He gives me the creeps."

"Yeah, well, government agents have to look tough," said Bert.

"Mrs. Burns didn't look like a government agent," said Flossie.

Bert smiled. "It's hard to look tough in a pink suit."

"She should take it to the cleaners," said Flossie. "Pink doesn't go with yellow smudges. I saw something yellow smeared on the back of her suit."

"That could be important. I wonder . . ." Bert muttered.

"Wonder what?" asked Flossie.

He was silent for a moment. Then he said, "I wonder what Mom will do to me if I don't get home right away. Come on, I'll race you home."

"Well, Nan, what do you think of your new

science teacher?" asked Mr. Bobbsey at dinner that evening.

"He's a new man," said Freddie. "Get it? New man?"

"We know he's *new* at school," Mr. Bobbsey replied. "But what's he like?"

"No, that's his name," explained Freddie. "Mr. *Newman.*"

Nan laughed. "Freddie was *trying* to make a joke. So far I like Mr. Newman better than Mrs. Kane."

"I can't wait to see all his inventions tomorrow," Freddie said. He reached out and gave Chief a pat on the head. The sheepdog pup was sitting next to him.

Freddie slowly took a piece of lamb chop off his plate and held it down next to his chair. Chief instantly snapped up the piece of meat.

Mrs. Bobbsey glanced at Freddie out of the corner of her eye. "I don't think Chief needs any more to eat tonight, Freddie," she said.

"That's right," Flossie said. "I just fed him."

Freddie gave Chief another pat. The puppy looked up at him and whined. "Sorry, pal," Freddie said. "It's against the rules."

Just then the phone rang. Mr. Bobbsey got up from the table. "Maybe it's the lumberyard," he said. "It's open late tonight."

A second later he came back. "Mary, it's for you. It's your editor."

Mrs. Bobbsey was a part-time reporter for the *Lakeport News.* She was used to her editor calling with new assignments at any time.

"Time for me to do some football practice," said Bert. "I've got to work on throwing the ball. Come on, Freddie. You can catch the ball."

"I'm already out the door," replied his younger brother. The two boys left.

"Oh no!" said Mrs. Bobbsey from the other room. "Not in Middle School!"

"What happened?" asked Flossie.

"Hush!" said Mr. Bobbsey. "Your mother's having a conversation. She'll tell you all about it later. Finish your peas."

"All right," Flossie grumbled, spearing a pea with her fork.

Mrs. Bobbsey finished talking and returned to the table. "I have to go over to the school," she announced. "There's been a break-in."

Nan looked worried. "Mom, did they steal the new computers?"

"No, sweetheart. It looks as if nothing was stolen," Mrs. Bobbsey said as she got her notebook and camera ready to go. "But Mr. Newman's classroom was broken into. The science lab was completely torn apart!"

4

The Man in the
Trench Coat

"Can I go with you?" asked Nan as her mother got out her car keys.

"Why would you want to?" Mrs. Bobbsey replied.

"It's my classroom," Nan explained.

Mrs. Bobbsey shook her head. "You have homework to do."

"I've already done it," said Nan. "Please, Mom, I might find a clue if you let me go."

"That's a matter for the police," Mrs. Bobbsey replied. "You've got to let them solve some crimes for themselves."

"But since it's my classroom I might see something they would miss."

"All right." Mrs. Bobbsey sighed. "But try not to get in the way."

"Thanks, Mom!"

As they headed toward the back door, Flossie jumped up. "Wait a minute!" she protested. "I want to go, too." She held up her plate. "See? I finished all my peas."

Mrs. Bobbsey laughed. "All right, Flossie. I know when I'm licked."

When they arrived at the Lakeport Middle School, two police cars were outside. Officer Tompkins was guarding the front door.

"Hello, Mrs. Bobbsey," he said. "This will make a sad article for your paper."

"Why is that?" asked Nan.

"Let me ask the questions, Nan," Mrs. Bobbsey said firmly. "What happened, Officer Tompkins?"

"Someone came in here and nearly demolished the school's science lab. It will cost thousands of dollars to replace the damaged equipment."

"That's terrible," replied Mrs. Bobbsey. "When did it happen?"

Officer Tompkins opened the door. "Sometime between six and seven this evening. I'll take you in, but don't touch anything."

"Can we come, too?" asked Flossie.

He smiled. "How could I keep two of the Bobbsey twins away from the scene of a serious crime like this?"

"Is he making fun of us?" Flossie whispered to her sister.

"I don't think so," answered Nan. "Anyway, at least he's letting us in."

Officer Tompkins led them through the dark halls.

"It's room four-oh-seven," said Nan.

"How do you know?" the policeman asked.

"It's my classroom."

"And besides," added Flossie, "it's the only room lit up on this floor."

"Very observant," he said cheerfully. "Nothing escapes the Bobbseys."

"That's us!" Flossie said proudly.

Inside the room were two school officials and another police officer. The police officer was sorting through the debris. Mrs. Bobbsey walked up to Mr. Jonas, the principal, and began to ask him about the damage. Nan and Flossie looked around the room.

"This place is a wreck," said Nan. "Who would do something like this?"

"Wow!" Flossie said, pointing. "The teacher's desk is upside down. And all the papers from his filing cabinets are spilled out."

"What a mess," Nan agreed. "Be careful of the broken glass."

"I will," promised Flossie. "I bet this lab equipment costs a lot of money."

"Yes, it does," said Mrs. Tylinski, the assistant principal. "We'll have to cut back our science program this year, I'm afraid."

"That's terrible," Nan said. Then her eye caught something written on the blackboard in big yellow letters: "TIME'S RUNNING OUT!"

"Flossie, look!" Nan said, pointing at the blackboard.

Flossie stared at the message. "What do you think it means?"

Nan shook her head, "I don't know. It's all very strange," she said. "First Bert and I see someone following Mr. Newman. Then there was that first threatening message. And now this one!"

Flossie sighed. "Poor Mr. Newman. It looks as if someone's out to get him."

"But *who?*" said Nan. "And why?" She looked at the blackboard again. She wondered if the same person had written both messages.

Nan decided she didn't know enough to tell the police yet.

"We've dusted the place for fingerprints," Officer Tompkins said to Mr. Jonas. "We'll be going now."

Mr. Jonas thanked the officers and ushered them out the door. Mrs. Bobbsey was talking to Mrs. Tylinski.

Flossie bent down and examined the debris on the floor. She picked something up and held it tightly in her hand.

"Come on, girls," said Mrs. Bobbsey. "I've got my story."

"But—" protested Flossie.

"No buts, young lady," her mother replied. "If you don't come quietly, I won't bring you out late again. It's already past your bedtime."

Flossie quietly trailed after her mother and Nan. She'd have to find a better time to mention the clue she'd found.

Nan, Bert, and Freddie were waiting outside of school the next day when Flossie ran up behind them.

"Hey!" she yelled. "I've got something to show you."

"What is it?" asked Nan.

"It's a clue I found at the science lab yesterday."

"Well, why didn't you show us sooner?" asked Bert.

"Because Mom sent me straight to bed last night, and this morning we all overslept and I didn't get a chance."

"Do you know who wrecked Mr. Newman's lab?" asked Nan.

"Not exactly," said Flossie. "But I'll know who it is when I see him."

"How do you know it's a him?" asked Bert.

"I don't," she said. "But when I find somebody who's missing this, I'll be sure!" Flossie held out a big black button in the palm of her hand.

"Great!" Freddie exclaimed. "Now we're getting somewhere! Bert was just telling us about that lady you met yesterday."

"Who?" asked Flossie.

"Julie Burns," said Bert. "Remember?"

"Sure," Flossie said. "She wanted to know about Mr. Newman. He used to work for her at— What was it, Bert?"

"DataComp Industries," he answered quickly. "They're a company that makes computers. I asked my computer teacher."

"Right," continued Flossie. "Julie Burns was wearing a pink suit. It was pretty, but it had yellow smears on the back."

"Yellow smears?" asked Nan.

"Yeah," said Flossie. "You know, like dust, or powder."

"Oh," said Nan.

"And Bert thinks she and Mr. Newman are spies," Flossie added.

"Spies!" said Nan and Freddie at the same time.

"Well," Bert said, trying to look confident, "Mrs. Burns did say it was a matter of security."

"That sounds pretty serious to me," Nan said softly.

"Hey, look!" shouted Freddie. "Here comes Mr. Newman now."

Bert pointed to a low brick wall a few feet away. "Let's wait behind that wall until he walks by. Then we'll follow him to see where he goes."

Moments later the science teacher walked past them, unaware he was being watched.

When he was safely past, Freddie stuck his head up over the wall. "He's halfway down the street."

"Let's go!" said Flossie. "This is fun!"

"Wait," whispered Nan. "Look over there, across the street. Do you recognize that man, Bert?"

Bert nodded his head. "It's the short guy in

the trench coat, the one we saw following Mr. Newman yesterday."

"But he's not following Mr. Newman now," said Freddie. "Mr. Newman's going in the opposite direction, toward his house."

"We'd better split up," Nan said. "Freddie and Bert, you follow Mr. Newman. Flossie and I will follow the guy in the trench coat."

Bert and Freddie raced away to catch up to Mr. Newman.

Nan and Flossie began to follow the man in the trench coat.

"That man sure looks weird," said Flossie.

"Just because he's wearing a trench coat when it isn't raining?"

"No, it's that hair! It looks as if he just got an electric shock." Flossie giggled.

"Not too loud, or he'll hear us. We're supposed to be following him without him knowing it."

"Look!" said Flossie in a low voice. "He dropped something."

The strange man kept on going.

Nan picked the object up off the sidewalk. "It's some kind of identification card."

"It's from DataComp!" said Flossie. She read the card out loud. " 'Rick Aaron, Engineer.' Does he drive a train?"

"No," said Nan. "An engineer can also be a person who builds things."

"I've figured it all out," Flossie said excitedly. "He's a spy, too!"

"But why would a spy be after Mr. Newman?" Nan stared at the plastic card in her hand.

"He's not after Mr. Newman anymore!" Flossie grabbed Nan's arm and pointed up the street.

Nan looked up and saw the strange man racing back in their direction. His eyes were wide and staring.

"He's not after Mr. Newman," Flossie cried. "He's after us!"

5

The Bigger They Are . . .

Nan wasn't sure what to do. But just as she decided they should run, the stranger called out. "Thank goodness you found it!"

"Did you lose this?" asked Nan, as the man reached them. "Are you Rick Aaron?"

A look of relief filled his face. "Yes," he said. "I must have dropped it."

Nan handed him the card.

"Thank you very much," replied Mr. Aaron. Nan noticed that he was sweating heavily. "I'd have been in a lot of trouble if I'd lost this. My boss is very strict."

"Oh?" said Nan. "Do you work for Julie Burns?"

"Yes," said Mr. Aaron with a frown. "Mrs.

Burns is the head of new projects at DataComp. How do you know her?"

Flossie smiled brightly. "Oh, we have an uncle who used to work at DataComp," she said.

"New projects?" Nan asked quickly. "Does that mean new inventions?"

"Yes, it does," Mr. Aaron replied.

Nan tried to get him to say more. "That must be real secret work."

"Yeah," Flossie interrupted. "A matter of security."

Rick Aaron looked at the girls. There was a strange expression on his face. "Yes, it is. But it won't matter to me much longer. I'm quitting in a few weeks anyway."

"Just like Mr. Newman?" asked Nan. "He used to work at DataComp."

"I know," said Mr. Aaron, nervously blinking his eyes. "He and I used to work together. He's brilliant. Do you know him?"

"He's her teacher," said Flossie. "So why were you—"

"Flossie," said Nan, deliberately interrupting her sister. "We don't want to bother Mr. Aaron any more."

"Thanks for finding my ID card," Rick Aaron said quickly. "Goodbye." He hurried around the corner.

Nan and Flossie walked back to their house. Bert and Freddie were standing on the corner of their street.

"If he knows Mr. Newman," said Flossie, "then why was he spying on him?"

"I don't know," replied Nan. "I'm not so sure I believe him, anyway."

"Believe who?" asked Bert.

"Mr. Newman just went straight home. What happened to that guy you were following?" asked Freddie.

Nan and Flossie explained.

Bert shook his head. "I don't know what to think."

"At least he had all his buttons," said Flossie.

"But where does that leave us?" asked Nan.

"Well," said Bert, "we've got Rick Aaron, who might be a spy. We have Julie Burns and Mr. Carroll, who might be spies, too."

"There was a break-in at the school," added Nan. "Secret messages and a lost button—"

"From a spy's coat, I bet!" Flossie added.

"And we have a new science teacher with a secret." Bert scratched his head. "It doesn't add up."

"I'd say that we have—nothing." Nan picked up her bookbag.

"And I'd say—" Bert leaned over and put an

arm around Freddie's shoulders. "I'd say it's time for our inside agent to go to work."

Freddie smiled as Bert began walking him up the street. "Your mission, Freddie Bobbsey, should you decide to accept it . . ."

The next afternoon Freddie Bobbsey knocked on Mr. Newman's front door.

Mr. Newman opened the door. "Come right in, Freddie," he said. "Everybody else is already here for the science club meeting."

"Sorry I'm late," said Freddie.

When Freddie took a seat in the living room, a small box on wheels bumped into his foot.

"I . . . am . . . sorry," said a stiff metallic voice coming from the box.

"What's that?" Freddie asked.

"It's a robot, silly," said Kimberly Bolton, one of Freddie's classmates. "I thought you knew everything, Freddie!"

"I know enough, Kimberly," Freddie said. He turned toward the science teacher. "What kind of robot is it?"

"It's one I built," explained Mr. Newman. "Robots are my hobby. Some of them are programmed to move around by themselves. Some have to be operated by remote control." He held up a small box. "This box controls the robot that bumped into you, Freddie. I programmed it to say a few words."

Freddie noticed several other small robots in the living room. Each one was different. One looked like a large metal doll. It hopped on four legs like a frog. Another rolled around in circles, guided by a wire that a girl was holding. One robot on the table was just a big arm. A red robot was trying to climb the stairs, but its legs were too short, and it kept falling back down.

"I wish I had a big robot," said Freddie. "Then it could beat up bullies for me."

"Robots are useful, but I don't think you should build one for that purpose," Mr. Newman said.

"I guess you're right," Freddie said.

"In any case," Mr. Newman said, "the robots we build in this science club won't be able to hurt people."

"Are we really going to build robots?" Freddie asked excitedly.

"That's the science club's first project," said a freckle-faced boy. "Mr. Newman's going to teach us how to build a real robot."

"A big one?" asked Freddie. "The ones you have are all pretty small. Do you have any big ones? Can we see them?"

Suddenly all six kids were begging to see bigger robots. Mr. Newman looked very uncomfortable. "Oh no. A big robot might be too dangerous," he said nervously. "All my robots are less than two feet high."

"Besides," added a little girl, "the smaller they are, the less they cost. Mr. Newman says we'll all have to chip in to pay for the robot."

"Oh," Freddie mumbled.

"Examine these robots in the living room for today and make notes, students," said Mr. Newman. "Next week we'll decide what we want our robot to do."

Freddie began playing with a small robot on wheels. It was shaped like a bucket and had a face painted on it. He pointed the robot toward a door on the other side of the room and turned it on.

Crash! The little robot bounced off the closed door and fell over.

"Can I open the door, Mr. Newman?" asked Freddie. "My robot needs more room to maneuver."

"I'd prefer that everyone stay in the living room, Freddie."

Suddenly Freddie heard a loud crash from the other side of the door.

"What's going on behind that door?" Freddie asked.

"Nothing," said Mr. Newman nervously. "Why do you ask?"

"I thought I heard a noise in the next room."

"Nonsense," the teacher replied. "There's so much noise in here I can barely hear you."

Freddie nodded and went back to playing with his robot. But as soon as Mr. Newman was looking in a different direction, Freddie leaned closer to the door.

Freddie was sure he could hear a loud clanking noise behind it. What was inside?

Then he heard an even louder crashing sound.

"What was that?" asked one child.

"I heard it, too!" said another.

Mr. Newman looked very nervous. "Probably just a truck going by."

Freddie could hear a rattling sound just on the other side of the door. Why was Mr. Newman pretending he couldn't hear all these sounds? Sure, it was noisy in the living room, but not *that* noisy.

Bam! Bam! Bam!

All the kids stopped what they were doing. Even Mr. Newman couldn't ignore the noises this time. They sounded like a table loaded with dishes smashing to the floor.

"Excuse me," said Mr. Newman. Pushing

past Freddie, he unlocked the door and quickly slid into the next room.

Freddie tried to peek in, but Mr. Newman slammed the door almost in his face.

"What's wrong with *him?*" asked Kimberly.

Mr. Newman returned a moment later. He locked the door behind him. "Sorry, kids. My dog was making all that noise."

"What kind of a dog do you have?" asked Freddie.

"Uh, a German shepherd," Mr. Newman answered. "Our science club meeting is over for today."

"But it's only four o'clock," protested Freddie.

"Don't forget—next week we'll decide what kind of robot we want to build," said the teacher, quickly pushing everyone out the front door.

"That does it," muttered Freddie Bobbsey to himself. "Mr. Newman's definitely hiding something. And I'm going to find out what it is." He raced home to tell Bert and his sisters what had happened at the science club meeting.

The next afternoon, Freddie and Flossie went over to Mr. Newman's house. Flossie carried a big tray of cookies.

"Now, don't forget my plan," said Freddie.

"And don't you forget that I baked these cookies myself," Flossie replied.

"With Mom's help," Freddie quickly reminded her.

"Anyway," said Flossie, "they're my favorite kind, chocolate fudge."

Flossie walked up to Mr. Newman's front door and rang the doorbell. Freddie ran around to the side of the house just as the door opened.

"Hello," said Mr. Newman. "What can I do for you?"

"I'm selling cookies," explained Flossie. "Would you like to buy some?"

Mr. Newman looked over his shoulder nervously. He was clutching several very large pieces of paper in his hand. "I'm busy right now. Could you come back later?"

"But my cookies won't be fresh then," said Flossie. "They're really good."

"I can't talk now," Mr. Newman said.

"I'll even give you a sample," she said, holding out the tray. "See? They're individually wrapped."

"I don't have time!" shouted Mr. Newman.

Startled, Flossie dropped the tray. Cookies spilled all over the porch.

Mr. Newman bent down to pick up the

cookies. Flossie bent over, too. She peeked at the papers Mr. Newman was holding.

Flossie could see the papers had drawings on them. Written in large letters on the top of one were the words *LSJ-33 Robot.*

"I'm sorry," said Mr. Newman, picking up the last cookie. "I didn't mean to frighten you."

"You didn't," said Flossie. "My hands just slipped. I'll still give you a free sample."

"Never mind," Mr. Newman answered irritably. "How much for all of them?"

"Three dollars," she answered.

"Here," said Mr. Newman, handing her the money. "Thank you and goodbye."

Flossie skipped down the steps. Freddie met her at the corner.

"Guess what I found out!" Freddie said excitedly.

"What?"

"While you were stalling Mr. Newman, I opened the window and peeked inside," he said. "I saw a person tied to a chair inside the locked room. He was tied up with a blanket over his head. Mr. Newman has a kidnapped prisoner!"

"Maybe it was a big robot," said Flossie.

"But Mr. Newman has only tiny robots," Freddie said. "Why do you think it was a big robot?"

"Because I saw some plans—you know, like the ones Daddy has sometimes," Flossie explained. "One of them said 'LSJ-thirty-three Robot.'"

"Then maybe it *was* a robot," said Freddie. "It never moved or anything."

"What did you say?" someone said behind them.

Freddie and Flossie spun around. A bald man was standing right behind them.

"Who are you?" asked Freddie.

Flossie leaned over to Freddie and whispered in his ear, "That's the creepy guy Bert and I saw with Julie Burns. Be careful!"

"I'm not spying on you," the man answered. "My name is Mr. Carroll, and I'm just curious to hear what you were saying about Mr. Newman. I noticed you were talking to him. Did he show you any of his robots?"

"No," said Freddie quickly. Government agent or not, he didn't trust this stranger.

Mr. Carroll looked at Flossie. "Aren't you the same little girl my boss spoke to the other day?"

"Yes, I am," Flossie answered.

"Then she told you how important this is." Mr. Carroll pulled his wallet from his pocket. He opened it and showed them a very official-looking ID card. "See, I'm David Carroll. I'm the assistant chief of security for DataComp. It's very important that you tell me what you saw in that house."

"I know," said Flossie proudly. "It's a matter of security."

Freddie glanced at Flossie. Then he turned back to Mr. Carroll. "Are you on some kind of spy mission?"

"Let's just say it's important that I know what you know," Mr. Carroll replied. He took a step toward the twins and leaned in close. "Now—tell me about the LSJ-thirty-three."

Suddenly Flossie's eyes went wide. One of the buttons on Mr. Carroll's coat was missing. And the others matched the one she had found in the science lab!

"Freddie," she whispered. "Let's get out of here. Quick!"

"Come on," said Mr. Carroll. "Tell me the truth. Has Mr. Newman built his big robot yet?"

Flossie and Freddie edged back. The bald man pushed forward. "Tell me what you know."

Flossie and Freddie exchanged glances. Suddenly Mr. Carroll held out his arms and blocked their path. "You're not going anywhere, kids, until you tell me about that robot."

6

A Mysterious Letter

Before Freddie and Flossie could think of what to do next, they saw Bert hurrying toward them.

"What's going on here?" said Bert firmly as he came up behind Mr. Carroll.

"Er, nothing at all," the bald man said hesitantly. He turned to face Bert. "I was just asking them some questions."

He took out his wallet again and showed Bert his ID card. "I'm Mr. Carroll. I'm the man who was with Mrs. Burns the other day."

"I remember," Bert said, nodding.

Mr. Carroll became very serious. "Look, kids, Mr. Newman took something that doesn't belong to him. Until we get it back it *is* a matter of security, as the little girl says. I hope we can trust you to tell no one about this. No one."

Without saying another word, Mr. Carroll turned around and walked away.

"Wow," said Freddie with a sigh. "This case is getting stranger and stranger."

"Are you two all right?" asked Bert.

"We're fine," Flossie replied. "He wanted to know what we knew about Mr. Newman's robot."

"Robot?" asked Bert.

"Yeah," Freddie explained. "Mr. Newman's building a large robot, and that guy wants to know about it."

"Not only that," said Flossie excitedly. "He was missing a button on his coat!"

"So what?" asked Freddie.

"Don't you remember?" Flossie said impatiently. "I found a button on the floor of the science lab. I bet Mr. Carroll was the one who wrecked the lab."

"Hang on to that button," said Bert. "It might prove that Mr. Carroll is the one threatening Mr. Newman.

"But *why* is he threatening him?" asked Flossie.

Suddenly Freddie snapped his fingers. "Maybe the robot Mr. Newman is building is so fantastic that everyone wants it. A super robot like that could be worth a lot of money. Maybe he stole the plans from DataComp."

Bert nodded his head. "That would explain why everyone is spying on Mr. Newman."

"That's why Mrs. Burns is after him!" Flossie exclaimed. "He's building a stolen robot."

"I've got a hunch you're right," said Bert. "And my hunches are never wrong."

"Oh really?" said Freddie. "I remember one time . . ."

Meanwhile, Nan was out in the woods working on her science project for Mr. Newman's class. Her subject was plants that grow in the water. Nan was walking along the muddy edge of Smith Pond, examining lily pads.

I wish I had worn my boots, she thought to herself as she squished through the mud.

Nan drew pictures of the various plants she saw growing in the water: reeds, water lilies, and cattails. She picked a few so she could draw them at home later.

Nan twisted around to get a freshly sharpened pencil out of her backpack. She looked up and saw a short man in a trench coat. It was Rick Aaron, the same person she'd seen spying on Mr. Newman.

Rick Aaron was about ten feet away, walking

among the trees. He was headed in her direction. Nan watched carefully as he came closer. What was he doing here? she wondered. Maybe he was going to Mr. Newman's house. It wasn't far away.

Nan scrambled behind a bush and watched as he slowly stepped closer and closer. She noticed that he had a bunch of papers in his hands.

Suddenly Mr. Aaron stumbled over a tree branch and nearly fell down. When he caught his balance, he turned and headed down another path.

Nan silently grabbed up her things and began tailing him. She followed him for a few minutes through the thick woods.

Then she spotted a piece of paper on the ground.

She picked it up. It was a photocopy of a letter from the Megatronics Security Company. The letter was addressed to Mr. Newman.

Nan looked up before reading it. Mr. Aaron had turned around and was looking right at her through his thick glasses.

"Hey, you!" he shouted. "This is the third time I've seen you. I think you're following me, and I want to know why!"

With that, Rick Aaron came running toward Nan. "You're going to tell me everything! Everything!"

7

Putting the Clues Together

Nan was terrified. Clutching the letter and her backpack, she quickly turned and ran. But she stopped dead when she reached Smith Pond. She glanced around, looking for a way to go. Ahead of her the pond became a muddy swamp. And to the right, there was a thick briar patch. There was no way Nan could get through those thorns without hurting herself.

Nan looked to her left and spotted a log spanning a narrow part of the pond.

"Come back here, you!" shouted Rick Aaron.

Nan didn't stop to think. She moved swiftly across the log, almost losing her balance before reaching the other side. She jumped off the log and kept right on running. She didn't look back.

Suddenly she heard a huge splash.

Glancing back, she saw Mr. Aaron in the water. He was too busy gathering up all the wet papers to continue following her any longer.

Nan cracked a smile as he stumbled around in the water. Then she sped home.

Freddie and Flossie were watching TV. Bert was in the backyard, mowing the lawn. She called them all together for a meeting.

"Look what I've got!" she said, showing them the paper Rick Aaron had dropped.

"Where did you get this?" Bert asked.

"From Rick Aaron," said Nan. "He was in the woods by Smith Pond and dropped it. He might have been sneaking around Mr. Newman's house this afternoon."

"What does it say?" Freddie asked eagerly.

"It's dated three weeks ago." Nan read it aloud. " 'Dear Mr. Newman. This is to let you know that Megatronics is interested in your offer. But we would like to see a demonstration before we set a price. Please let us know when you can be ready.' "

Bert let out a low whistle. "It's signed by the president of the company."

"Ready to demonstrate what?" asked Flossie.

"Probably that big robot," Bert replied. "The LSJ-thirty-three."

"So what do we do now?" Freddie asked, bouncing on the sofa. He was really excited about the new clue.

"I'm not sure," said Nan. She studied the letter for a moment. "I wonder why this is only a photocopy?"

"What do you mean?" asked Bert.

"I think Rick Aaron stole this from Mr. Newman's house," said Nan.

"So?" Freddie leaned in to look at the letter.

"Wouldn't Mr. Newman have the original letter?" Nan asked.

"Yeah." Bert frowned. "So why does Rick Aaron have a copy?"

"He said he was Mr. Newman's friend at DataComp," Flossie offered.

"If he *is* Mr. Newman's friend, why was he following him?" Nan was getting confused. There seemed to be plenty of questions and no answers. "And Mr. Aaron didn't want Mr. Newman to recognize him."

"It looks like everybody is after Mr. Newman!" said Freddie, throwing up his hands.

"Yeah," Flossie agreed. "Mrs. Burns, Mr. Carroll, and Mr. Aaron."

"The question is," said Nan, "who's a crook and who isn't a crook?"

"Well, there's only one way to find out," said Bert. "We've got to catch somebody doing something wrong."

"And the best place to do that," said Nan, "is at Mr. Newman's house."

"But tomorrow's Saturday, and Mr. Newman will be home," Flossie objected.

"No, he won't," explained Nan. "He told our class he'll be cleaning up the science lab tomorrow. Mr. Aaron will have a perfect opportunity to break into Mr. Newman's again, if he's looking for the plans to the robot."

"What if Mr. Newman comes home while we're watching the house?"

"You and I will just have to go to the science lab and delay him," replied Nan.

"That sounds like fun," said Flossie.

"I'll talk to him about my science project," said Nan. "Too bad I dropped my plants when Mr. Aaron was chasing me. Asking him about those would have been a good excuse to be there."

"Take some of the plants from my aquarium," said Bert. "They've been growing so fast they're crowding out the fish."

"Great idea," said Nan. "Thanks."

"So tomorrow I'll be at Mr. Newman's, waiting for Mr. Aaron to strike," said Bert.

"Me too," added Freddie.

"Right," Bert said with a nod. "We'll wait near Mr. Newman's house and follow this Aaron guy to see where he goes when he leaves."

"I have a feeling that if we catch him with the plans to the robot we'll solve this whole mystery," said Nan.

Bert nodded. "Tomorrow," he said, "we'll get to the bottom of all this."

On Saturday morning, Nan and Flossie went to the science lab at school. Mr. Newman was busy setting up some new equipment on one of the lab tables.

"Hi, Mr. Newman," said Nan.

"What are you doing at school on a Saturday?" Mr. Newman asked in a surprised voice.

"I found this plant in the water at Smith Pond, but I can't figure out what it is."

"Let me look it up in my field guide," said the teacher.

While he looked up the plant from Bert's aquarium, Nan and Flossie walked around the room.

"Are you sure you got this plant from Smith Pond?" asked Mr. Newman, flipping through the book. "It doesn't resemble any freshwater plant I've ever seen."

Flossie started to speak, but Nan signaled her

to be quiet. "Oh yes, it's from there. I found it after school yesterday."

Mr. Newman searched through book after book. Nan watched him for a moment, then decided to mention Rick Aaron.

"Yesterday, when I was at the pond, I saw a strange man," said Nan, curious to see Mr. Newman's reaction.

"That's nice," said Mr. Newman, only half listening.

"The man dropped a letter from the Megatronics Company."

"What?" shouted Mr. Newman, dropping a heavy field guide. "What are you talking about?"

"This!" Nan said. She handed the copy of the letter to the science teacher.

"Oh no!" Mr. Newman cried as he sat down in a chair by one of the student desks. "This is terrible. I had no idea anyone knew about this letter. I've worked on my invention for ten years. I've kept it a secret until now. How could someone have found out about it?"

"We know who it is," said Nan.

"Who?" Mr. Newman asked.

"It was Rick Aaron," Nan said. "He used to work with you, right?"

Mr. Newman stared at her. He had a shocked expression on his face.

"I can't believe Rick Aaron would steal anything," said Mr. Newman slowly. "He was one of my best friends at DataComp."

"Why did you quit working at DataComp, Mr. Newman?"

"Because Megatronics said they were interested in buying my invention—"

"What is your invention, Mr. Newman?" asked Flossie.

"A robot," Mr. Newman replied. *My* robot. One of the largest, most advanced robots ever built. And Megatronics was going to buy it. All they wanted was to see a demonstration."

"You mean you're really building a man-sized robot?" said Nan.

"Yes." Mr. Newman looked really worried. "I knew I needed more time to work on the robot. Teaching would give me that opportunity. So I quit DataComp. I thought I had kept this a secret, even from Rick. But now—"

"I don't think you should worry too much," said Nan. "It looked as if Mr. Aaron was heading for your house yesterday. But he got side-tracked when he fell into the pond."

"That means he might go back today to look for a set of the plans. Rick could be at my house right now. I've got to go home and make sure those plans are still there."

"Don't worry," said Nan. "Our brothers,

Freddie and Bert, are already at your house. They're going to follow Rick Aaron if he comes around again."

"Oh no," gasped Mr. Newman. "We've got to hurry. If Rick really is out to steal my invention, all my work will be ruined. I only hope we can get there in time!"

8

Trapped!

Meanwhile, Bert and Freddie had just arrived on Mr. Newman's block. They quickly moved toward his house, ducking behind trees to keep out of sight.

"What if Rick Aaron doesn't come back?" asked Freddie. "I don't want to wait here all day."

"If you don't have patience, you'll never grow up to be a great detective," said Bert.

"If I don't have patients, I won't be a doctor, either," Freddie replied. "Ha, ha!"

"Ugh! Your puns are awful."

"Those are the best kind," bragged Freddie. "Hey, why don't we go inside Mr. Newman's house and wait for the burglar there?"

"First of all, it's against the law to enter a house without permission," began Bert, "and second, the door's probably locked."

"Maybe it's not," said Freddie. He quickly ran up to the front door and turned the doorknob.

"Well?" asked Bert. "Is it locked?"

"Yeah," said Freddie. He looked a little disappointed.

"I thought so," said Bert. "Let's make sure everything's all right in back of the house. Then we'll find a good place to hide and keep watch."

As the two boys reached the backyard Bert stopped suddenly.

"Did you hear something?" he asked.

"I didn't hear anything," Freddie replied, shrugging his shoulders.

"That's funny . . ." Bert stared off into the woods beyond Mr. Newman's picket fence. "I thought I heard someone—"

"Look!" Freddie interrupted. "The kitchen door is wide open!"

Bert blinked his eyes. "You're right. Mr. Newman wouldn't lock the front door and leave this one open."

"So who opened it?" Freddie wondered. "Maybe we ought to investigate."

After thinking for a moment, Bert agreed. "I

guess if it's wide open, we might as well go in and make sure nothing's wrong."

"What if somebody's inside?" asked Freddie.

Bert smiled sheepishly. "Then we run like crazy. Come on."

Bert boldly walked up to the open door with Freddie right behind. He knocked on the door frame.

"Hello, Mr. Newman?" said Freddie.

"Mr. Newman?" Bert called in a louder voice.

No one answered.

Bert knocked again. Still no answer.

"He *can't* be here," said Freddie. "He would have answered us by now."

The two boys entered Mr. Newman's house. No one seemed to be inside. They slowly walked through the kitchen, along a hallway, and into the living room.

"Hey," said Freddie, "look at this." He held up a large badge he'd found on a table. It was made of plastic with thin metal strips on the back. There were three words written on the front.

" 'RP Security Badge,' " he read aloud. "It's pretty heavy for such a small piece of plastic. I wonder why Mr. Newman has a whole box of them?" Freddie asked, picking up a few more.

"Maybe he stole them," said Bert. "He's been

so secretive, I'm not sure I trust him. What's in there?" Bert pointed to the closed door in the living room.

"That's where I saw the man who was tied up," said Freddie. "Mr. Newman claimed he kept his dog in there."

Bert turned the knob—and the door swung open. He turned to Freddie. "I thought you said it was locked."

"It was before. Hey, look at that!" yelled Freddie, peering into the room.

"What is it?" asked Bert.

"A giant robot!" Freddie said. "Keep away from it, Bert. It might be dangerous."

A large silver-colored mechanical man stood in the middle of the room. It had a smooth dome-shaped head. Its arms ended in big clamps for hands.

"Intruder alert!" said the robot in a loud metallic voice. Its eyes began to flash. "Leave this area at once." Then it rolled toward Bert.

"Hey, the door was open," Bert tried to explain to the advancing robot. "We didn't mean any harm."

"This area is off limits!" came the voice from the robot's speaker. It raised one arm, blocking their path to the door.

"Get out of my way, then," yelled Bert. "We want to get out of here."

"Quit picking on my brother," Freddie shouted.

Bert tried to dodge around the robot, but it held up its other arm. Both of the robot's clamplike hands snapped at Bert's head.

"Run, Bert," yelled Freddie.

"I'm trying, I'm trying!" Bert ducked below the robot's arms. He turned and ran into the living room. The robot rolled after him.

Bert climbed over a couch. "Why isn't it chasing you, Freddie?" Bert called out.

"I don't know," Freddie said, as the robot rolled around him toward the couch. "Maybe it's this badge I'm holding."

"Throw me one!"

Freddie tossed one of the security badges to Bert.

Just barely catching it, Bert waved the odd-looking badge in front of the menacing robot.

"It stopped!" exclaimed Freddie.

"Now I get it," said Bert. He came out from behind the couch. "When the robot's turned on, it will attack anyone who isn't wearing one of these badges."

"This robot must be what I saw when I peeked in the window the other day," said Freddie. "I guess Mr. Newman isn't a kidnapper after all."

Bert gave the robot a friendly pat on its metal chest. "It had me fooled, too."

"Mr. Newman sure is smart," said Freddie. "I'd like to be an inventor like him when I grow up."

"I'd say there are still a few bugs in this robot's system. Unless Mr. Newman just forgot to turn it off before he went to the lab today. It could have run out the back door and hurt someone. Can you turn it off?"

"Sure," bragged Freddie. "I can operate any machine in the world. Well, almost any machine."

"Just take care of this one," replied Bert.

Freddie studied the robot for a few minutes. Finally he found a small switch in the robot's back. He flicked the switch, turning the robot off. Then he heard someone in the kitchen. "Someone's here, Bert."

"It might be Rick Aaron!"

"We'd better hide until he goes away," said Bert. "We're not supposed to be here, you know."

The two Bobbsey boys quickly hid behind the couch.

"We should have locked the back door," whispered Freddie.

"Be quiet," Bert whispered. "And duck down."

They heard someone approaching the living room doorway. "Newman, we've come to talk to you," a voice called out.

"That's Mrs. Burns," Freddie whispered.

"Maybe he's gone out for the day," a male voice suggested.

And Mr. Carroll is with her, thought Bert.

"Then we'll wait until he comes back," Mrs. Burns said. "I'm not wasting any more time."

Freddie and Bert didn't make a sound. They could hear footsteps as Mrs. Burns and Mr. Carroll entered the room.

Suddenly Freddie sneezed.

"Quiet!" Bert whispered.

"I can't help it! *Achoo!*"

"Okay, you two!" ordered Julie Burns. "Come out from behind that couch. Right now!"

Bert and Freddie stood up.

"Aha!" said Mrs. Burns. "What have we here? Two boys who've broken into Mr. Newman's house. The police will be most interested."

Freddie glared at them. "We *didn't* break in," he said.

David Carroll laughed loudly. "Oh, really? Why should we believe you?"

"I'd say you boys are in big trouble," Mrs. Burns added.

"We're not scared of you," Bert said. "We're telling the truth."

"We'll see about that," said Julie Burns. "Call the police, Mr. Carroll, and tell them we've just caught two thieves."

9

Race Against Time

Nan and Flossie climbed into Mr. Newman's car. "Hurry," said Flossie. "Our brothers might be in danger."

"We'll be there in five minutes," promised Mr. Newman. He started the car and pulled out of the school parking lot.

"Oh no!" cried Nan. "Stop the car!"

"What's wrong?" asked Mr. Newman.

Nan pointed. "There's Rick Aaron!"

Mr. Newman pulled over to the curb. "I'm going to have it out with him right now!"

"Shouldn't you go for the police?" asked Flossie. "He could be dangerous."

"I can handle this," said Mr. Newman as he jumped out of the car.

Nan and Flossie got out of the car and hurried after him.

"Rick!" shouted Mr. Newman.

Aaron spun around. "Peter!" he cried. "What are you doing here?"

"Never mind that," snapped the teacher. "Why are you spying on me?"

"I don't know what you're talking about," Mr. Aaron replied nervously.

"Witnesses can prove that you've been following me," Mr. Newman said angrily. "I could have you arrested."

Mr. Aaron held up his hand. "All right, all right, I admit I've been following you all week."

"Why?" asked Mr. Newman. "I thought you were my friend."

"I am," Rick Aaron said. He seemed very upset and confused.

"Then tell me what you were up to," said Mr. Newman.

"I—I—" Rick Aaron stammered at first. Then he took a deep breath and looked Mr. Newman in the eyes. "I was trying to find out if you were a thief!"

"A what?" Mr. Newman exclaimed.

"A thief," Rick Aaron repeated. "I was trying

to get up enough nerve to talk to you. You see, someone told me you had stolen something from DataComp."

"Was it Mrs. Julie Burns?" asked Nan.

"Why, yes, it was," Mr. Aaron said. "How did you know?"

"Partly because she told us the same thing," Nan answered.

Flossie looked up at her sister. "You've figured something out, haven't you, Nan?" Flossie said excitedly.

"Maybe," Nan said softly. "Did Mrs. Burns show you a letter, Mr. Aaron?"

"Yes." Rick Aaron looked genuinely surprised. He turned back to Mr. Newman. "It was from Megatronics. Julie said you had stolen the plans for a robot from DataComp and were going to sell them to Megatronics. She and David Carroll asked me what I knew about the project."

"They thought you knew about it because we were friends," said Mr. Newman.

"I couldn't believe that you were a thief. So—"

"You started following Mr. Newman all over town," Flossie interrupted. "You weren't very good, though. We saw you a couple of times. You should take lessons from my brother Bert."

"You saw me following Peter?" asked Mr.

Aaron. "What are you kids, detectives or something?"

"That's right!" Flossie said proudly.

"I knew someone was after my invention," said Mr. Newman. He was still very upset. "Especially when I received those two messages on the blackboard. But now Julie believes I stole the plans from DataComp!"

"Not really, Mr. Newman." Nan smiled. "I think Mrs. Burns is after your invention for herself."

"What?" Mr. Newman exclaimed.

"That's right," Nan continued. "The night the lab was wrecked, Flossie found a button. Later she discovered that it belonged to Mr. Carroll's coat. He and Mrs. Burns were together outside your house."

"I bet you never invited him into the lab, did you, Mr. Newman?" asked Flossie.

"No, I never did." The science teacher was slowly beginning to understand.

Nan continued adding up the other clues. "Flossie also spotted yellow smears on Mrs. Burns's suit."

"Her pink one," Flossie added. "Pink's my favorite color."

"Not now, Floss," Nan said quickly. "The yellow smears were chalk marks. Mrs. Burns wrote those messages. It's been her all along.

She's probably been telling other engineers at DataComp that you're a crook. She wanted to get information about your robot so she could steal it."

Mr. Newman nodded his head. "Julie Burns is a very ambitious person. She'll stop at nothing to get what she wants. And neither will David Carroll. That robot is very valuable."

"I think we should go to Mr. Newman's house right away," Flossie said. "Freddie and Bert are there. They might run into trouble if those two are crooks."

"They're crooks all right," agreed Mr. Aaron. "Let's go."

"I hope we're not too late," said Flossie.

"Don't worry," Nan said. "I'm sure nothing bad will happen." But Nan didn't feel as confident as she sounded.

"I certainly hope you're right," said Mr. Newman grimly. "Because if you're not—"

10

Robot Rescue

Bert and Freddie sat on the sofa in Mr. Newman's living room.

Mr. Carroll reached for the telephone.

"Wait a minute, David," ordered Mrs. Burns. "Maybe we can make a deal with our little thieves."

"What kind of deal?" asked Bert.

"If you help us carry that robot out to the car, we'll let you go."

"We can go any time we want," said Freddie defiantly.

"Just try it," threatened Mr. Carroll. "You'll find out who's going where. Now grab that robot and don't drop it. You two take the bottom, and we'll take the arms."

"We'd better do what he says," Bert muttered.

"You'd better do *exactly* as you're told," said Mrs. Burns. She grabbed one of the robot's arms. "I didn't know it would be this big."

The four of them tried to lift the robot, but it was too heavy.

As the two adults discussed the problem, Bert whispered to Freddie, "If the plans for this robot belonged to them, how come they didn't know what size it would be?"

"Yeah," said Freddie slowly. "I bet they've never seen the plans before."

"And," said Bert, "how did they know there were two of us behind the couch?"

"That's right," said Freddie. "They must have seen us come in here."

"They're probably the ones who unlocked the back door," Bert added.

Both boys suddenly realized that they were really trapped with a couple of crooks.

"Too bad this robot can't roll out of here under its own power," said Mrs. Burns.

Bert and Freddie exchanged glances.

"It *can*," volunteered Bert.

"Bert!" Freddie cried. "Don't tell them about the—"

"What's this?" asked Mrs. Burns, her eyes

narrowing with interest. "Can you control the robot?"

"Sure," Bert said. "Just turn it on and *tell* it what you want it to do. Right, Freddie?"

Freddie nodded. "Right."

"Where's the switch?" asked Mr. Carroll.

Freddie pointed. "Right here."

Mr. Carroll threw the switch.

"Intruder alert! Intruder alert!"

Freddie and Bert jumped back. The robot swung around on its barrel-shaped body and grabbed Mr. Carroll around the waist with one arm. Then it turned and snatched a shocked-looking Julie Burns up in the other arm.

"You little rats," snarled Mr. Carroll. "Why didn't the robot attack you?"

"We're wearing our badges," said Bert. "Did we forget to give you one?"

"Too bad," said Freddie.

Just then Mr. Newman raced through the front door with Nan, Flossie, and Rick Aaron. "What's going on here?" the teacher asked.

"They wanted to steal your robot, Mr. Newman," Bert explained. "But we stopped them."

Suddenly the robot started clanking toward Nan and Flossie!

"Here—wear these badges, everybody," said Freddie.

"Don't give Mrs. Burns or Mr. Carroll a badge," said Mr. Newman. "At least, not until the police get here."

"I'll call them right away," said Nan.

"And I'll wait outside for them," Flossie added.

Mr. Newman and Mr. Aaron put on their plastic badges. "This is quite an invention," said Mr. Aaron. "I can see why Julie wanted to steal it. You'll be able to make millions on it, Peter."

"Those millions could have been mine," said Julie Burns, as she tried to wriggle out of the robot's grip. "These dreadful children spoiled everything."

Mr. Carroll didn't say anything. He just stared down at the floor.

"If you ask me, Mr. Newman's robot was the real hero," said Freddie. "We just helped."

Just then, the police arrived. Flossie showed them in, and Freddie handed them badges.

Freddie, Nan, and Bert quickly explained everything to Officer Tompkins.

"So these are the two who wrecked the school lab," said Officer Tompkins. "I'll be glad to put them behind bars."

"You can't prove it," yelled Mrs. Burns.

"Oh yes we can," Nan replied. "I'm sure the police will find traces of chalk on your suit.

And don't forget Mr. Carroll's missing button. That's evidence, too."

"Forget it," snapped Mr. Carroll, speaking for the first time. "You can't prove anything."

"Don't be too sure," said Officer Tompkins. "We found some fingerprints in the lab that might just match yours. And even if we don't, attempting to steal Mr. Newman's robot is going to get you into enough trouble."

"We weren't stealing it. Those boys were," Mrs. Burns said quickly.

Mr. Newman laughed.

"What's so funny?" grumbled David Carroll.

"My robot is designed to videotape everything it sees," Mr. Newman said proudly. He pushed a button on the robot, and a tiny screen popped out of its chest. Mr. Newman pressed another button. There was the whirring sound of a tape rewinding. Then the screen played back exactly what had happened.

"But the robot was turned off," said Mrs. Burns. "How could it have taped us?"

"Special security code," said Mr. Newman. "If the robot isn't turned off properly, the camera keeps rolling."

"Don't arrest me," screamed Mr. Carroll. "She did it," he said, pointing to Mrs. Burns. "She paid me to wreck the lab."

"Shut up," snarled Mrs. Burns.

"No, I won't," Mr. Carroll continued. "I don't want to go to jail for your crazy scheme."

Rick Aaron turned to Mr. Newman. "I always suspected you were working on something big. I'm glad it's going to work out for you."

"Good," said Mr. Newman. "Maybe you'd like to help me build more robots."

"Sure," Mr. Aaron replied. "I'd love to."

"I have all the information I need," said Officer Tompkins, closing his notebook. "All right, Mr. Newman, order your robot to let them go."

Mr. Newman pinned radio badges on the criminals. Instantly the robot released them, and two police officers led Mrs. Burns and Mr. Carroll away.

"Good riddance," said Flossie. "I knew they were guilty all the time."

"I wasn't sure," said Bert. "Everybody was running around trying to hide something."

"Nobody's perfect," said Mr. Newman.

Freddie chuckled. "Nobody except your robot!"

"A very efficient machine," said Officer Tompkins. "I could use a robot like that on the police force!"

"You'd better be careful," said Nan. "It might replace you."

Officer Tompkins eyed the robot carefully. "It looks strong, all right, but I don't think it has the judgment to be a good police officer."

"Or the brains to be a good detective," teased Nan.

"In this case," said Mr. Newman, "it took *four* good detectives—all of them named Bobbsey. I could never invent a robot to replace you!"